Here's what kids, parents, and teachers have to say to Ron Roy, author of the A to Z Mysteries series:

"My teacher asked me which of your books was my favorite. I told him they were all so good they were all my favorite."—Jackie D.

"I have never been hooked on to a series as much as this one."—Donald M.

"You are such a good author, I think that every child and grown-up should read your books." —Olivia M.

"My favorite series is definitely, no doubt, A to Z Mysteries!"—Jordan C.

"Thank you so very much for allowing my child to peek into a world of adventure." —Amber B.

"My students find the books extremely exciting, and they can't put them down." —Shirley K.

This book is dedicated to Matthew Johnson.
—R.R.

To Tim, thanks for posing!
—J.S.G.

www.randomhouse.com/kids
www.ronroy.com

Library of Congress Cataloging-in-Publication Data
Roy, Ron.
The unwilling umpire / by Ron Roy ; illustrated by John Steven Gurney. — 1st ed.
  p.   cm. — (A to Z mysteries)   "A stepping stone book."
SUMMARY: When the umpire at the baseball game fund-raiser is accused of stealing a
collection of autographed baseballs, Dink, Josh, and Ruth Rose try to prove his
innocence.
ISBN 0-375-81370-5 (trade) — ISBN 0-375-91370-X (lib. bdg.)
[1. Baseballs—Fiction.   2. Mystery and detective stories.]   I. Gurney, John, ill.
II. Title.   III. Series: Roy, Ron, 1940- . A to Z mysteries.
PZ7.R8139Un 2004   [Fic]—dc21   2003002663

Printed in the United States of America   10 9 8 7 6 5 4 3 2 1   First Edition

A to Z Mysteries®

The Unwilling Umpire

by Ron Roy

illustrated by
John Steven Gurney

A STEPPING STONE BOOK™

Random House New York

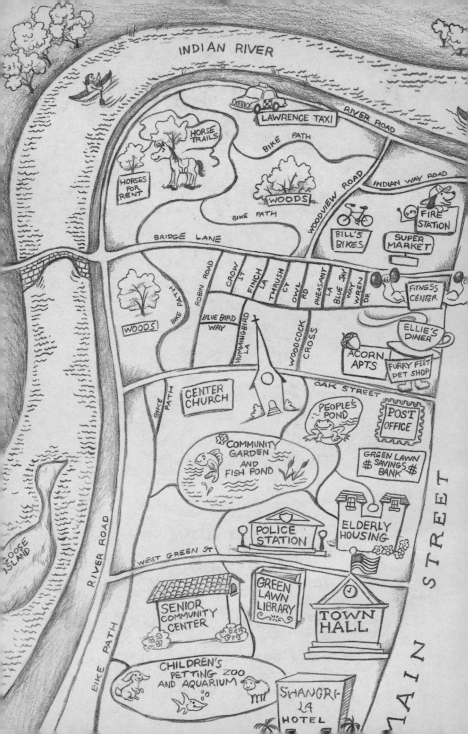

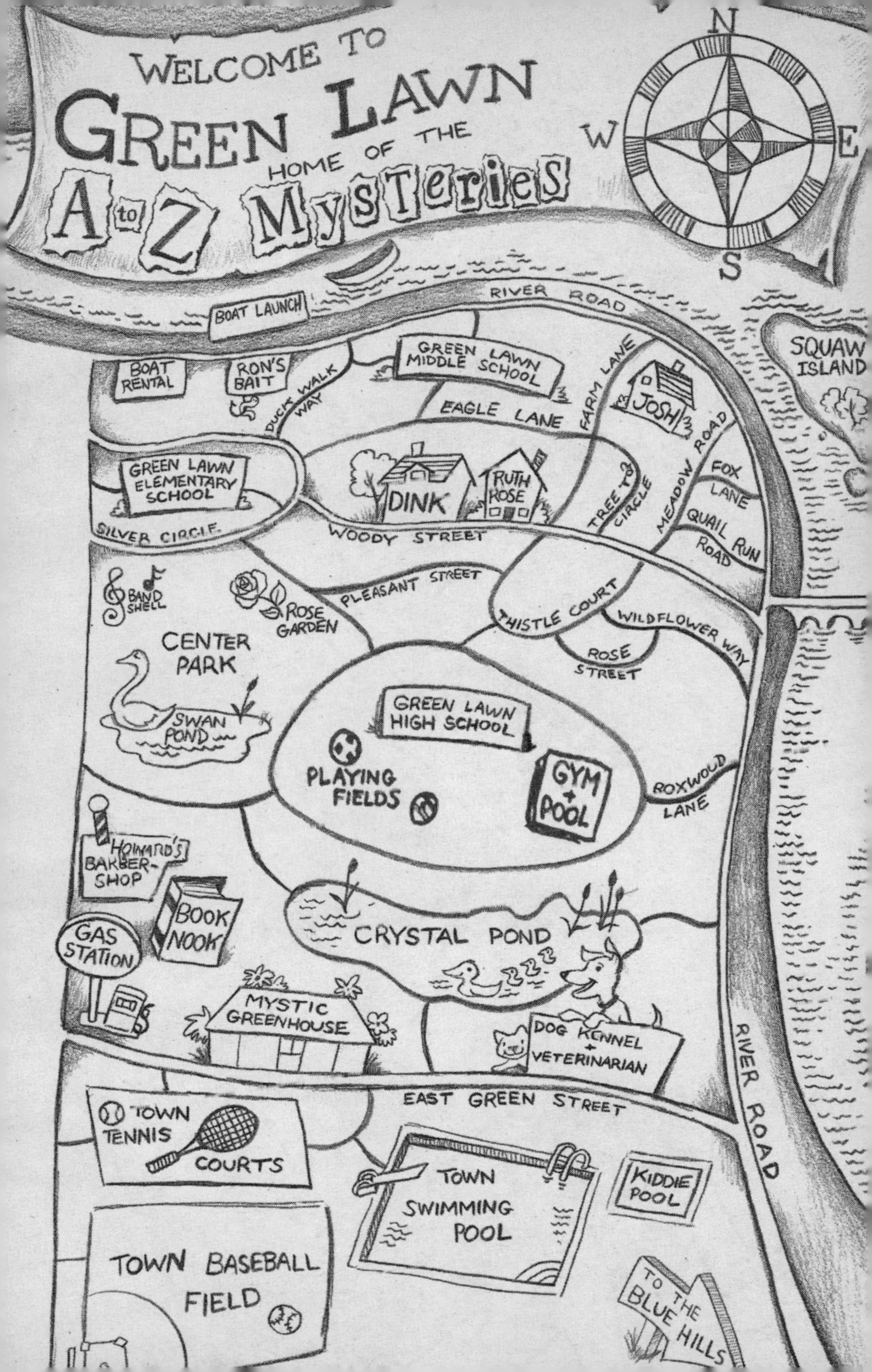
WELCOME TO
GREEN LAWN
HOME OF THE
A to Z MysTeries
N
W
E
S
RIVER ROAD
BOAT LAUNCH
SQUAW ISLAND
BOAT RENTAL
RON'S BAIT
DUCK WALK WAY
GREEN LAWN MIDDLE SCHOOL
FARM LANE
JOSH
EAGLE LANE
MEADOW ROAD
GREEN LAWN ELEMENTARY SCHOOL
DINK
RUTH ROSE
TREE CIRCLE
FOX LANE
QUAIL RUN ROAD
SILVER CIRCLE
WOODY STREET
BAND SHELL
ROSE GARDEN
PLEASANT STREET
THISTLE COURT
WILDFLOWER WAY
ROSE STREET
CENTER PARK
SWAN POND
GREEN LAWN HIGH SCHOOL
PLAYING FIELDS
GYM + POOL
ROXWOLD LANE
HOWARD'S BARBER-SHOP
BOOK NOOK
GAS STATION
CRYSTAL POND
MYSTIC GREENHOUSE
DOG KENNEL + VETERINARIAN
RIVER ROAD
EAST GREEN STREET
TOWN TENNIS COURTS
TOWN SWIMMING POOL
KIDDIE POOL
TOWN BASEBALL FIELD
TO THE BLUE HILLS

CHAPTER 1

CRACK!

The baseball popped into the warm June air and rose slowly toward the sky. The crowd leaped to its feet, yelling, "Run! Run!"

Mr. Dillon, the school principal, dropped the bat and raced toward first base.

Dink, Josh, and Ruth Rose were sitting in the front row of bleacher seats.

Dink's full name was Donald David Duncan, but his friends called him Dink.

"Having a baseball game to raise

money was a great idea," Ruth Rose said.

"Yeah," said Josh. "We have fun raising funds!"

The kids in Green Lawn had sold enough tickets to fill the bleachers at the town baseball field. The money would go to Camp Challenge, a summer camp for kids with special needs.

Out in center field, Josh's mom watched the baseball as it started to fall. She raised her glove and the ball dropped neatly into it.

Mr. Dillon was out! He trotted back toward home plate.

"I didn't know my mom could catch like that!" Josh said.

Dink grinned at Josh. "Too bad she couldn't teach *you* how," he said, giving Josh an elbow in the side.

"Great catch, Mom!" Josh yelled.

"Gentlemen, yer out!" yelled Pete Unkenholz, the umpire at home plate, motioning with his thumb. "Ladies, yer up!"

Pete was a tall, friendly guy with spiky blond hair. He was a good worker, too. He had helped set up the bleachers for the game.

Josh's mom's catch was the third out for the men's team. The women ran off the field, high-fiving each other. The men began to take their positions on the field, joking with the female players.

Josh turned to Ruth Rose. "Want to make a bet the men beat the women?" he asked.

Ruth Rose nodded, making her black, curly hair bounce. She liked to dress all in one color. Today she wore red from her headband down to her high-top sneakers.

"Sure, I'll bet you an ice cream cone that the women win," Ruth Rose said to Josh.

Josh flashed a grin. "You're on!" he

said, shaking Ruth Rose's hand.

The three kids watched the men take their positions. Their friend Mr. Thaddeus Pocket was head coach. He walked around the field, chatting with the players.

"How did Mr. Pocket learn so much about baseball?" Dink asked.

"He told me he played a lot in college," Josh said.

"It was great of him to bring some of the baseballs from his collection to the game today," Ruth Rose said.

"Yeah! I guess they're worth a lot of money," Dink added. "He let me hold the one signed by Babe Ruth!"

"Cool! I'm named after a famous baseball player!" Ruth Rose said.

"Ha!" Josh said. "I think they named a candy bar after him, too."

Six of Mr. Pocket's autographed baseballs were on display in the clubhouse. Everyone who bought a ticket to the game had a chance to admire them in the locked case.

The men were all in their field positions. Ellie was up first on the women's team. She grabbed a bat and headed for the batter's box. Pete smiled at Ellie and gave her a thumbs-up.

"Pete seems like a nice guy," Dink said. "I'm glad he volunteered to ump."

"Where did he come from?" Josh asked. "He just showed up a couple of weeks ago, right?"

Dink shrugged. "I don't know, but everyone seems to like him a lot."

"He sure is big," Ruth Rose observed. "Look how he towers over Ellie!"

Pete threw the ball to the men's pitcher, Mr. Linkletter. The scoreboard read: MEN 1, WOMEN 0.

"Play ball!" Pete yelled.

Ellie stepped up to the batter's box. Everyone cheered as she got ready for the first pitch from Mr. Linkletter.

Behind Ellie, Jake, a local firefighter, was catching. He crouched with his mitt in front of his chin.

The pitch was low, but Ellie swung anyway. She missed and the ball zinged into Jake's waiting glove.

"Strike one!" Pete announced as Jake tossed the ball to the pitcher. Mr. Linkletter wound up and threw his next pitch. This one was high, but Ellie swung and caught part of the ball. It skipped down the first-base line. Lucky O'Leary fielded the ball in foul territory and whipped it back to Mr. Linkletter.

"Strike two!"

The spectators jumped to their feet for the third pitch. Everyone was yelling, whistling, or clapping.

Pete raised his arms for quiet.

Mr. Linkletter's third pitch was right in the strike zone. Ellie swung with all her might.

CRACK! The ball soared over Mr.

Linkletter's head, dropped, and rolled between Officer Fallon's legs in center field.

Ellie took off. By the time Officer Fallon ran down the ball and snapped it to Lucky O'Leary at first, Ellie was rounding second base. Lucky threw to Doc Henry at third.

But Lucky's throw was wide.

When Doc lunged for the ball, Ellie made third base and kept running. With legs pumping and arms swinging, she thundered across home plate.

"Safe!" shouted Pete, throwing his arms wide.

Everyone leaped into the air and yelled. Ellie had scored the first run for the women!

The scoreboard now read: MEN 1, WOMEN 1.

CHAPTER 2

"It's a tie!" Ruth Rose said. "Mmm, I can taste that ice cream cone, Josh!"

"Boy, the men are lousy fielders," Josh grumbled. "My grandmother can catch better!"

Just then Pete Unkenholz started sneezing. He wiped his eyes, sneezed again, then turned to say something to the catcher. After a few seconds, Pete headed toward the clubhouse.

As Pete passed Dink, Josh, and Ruth Rose, he stopped for a second. "Darn allergies," the young man said. His eyes were red, and he was taking deep breaths.

Pete trudged toward the clubhouse. The kids watched Mr. Pocket walk over to home plate.

"What's going on?" they heard him ask the catcher.

"He went to get his allergy medicine," Jake told Mr. Pocket.

Mr. Pocket made an announcement over the public-address system. The crowd relaxed and waited for the game to continue. But when Pete hadn't returned after five minutes, people began to wonder what was going on.

"I'm going to use the boys' room," Josh said. "Be right back."

Josh jogged to the clubhouse while the crowd waited for Pete to return.

Suddenly Josh came racing back to the bleachers. He slid in next to Dink, out of breath.

"What's up?" Ruth Rose asked.

"You're not gonna believe this!" Josh whispered to his friends. "Mr. Pocket's autographed baseballs—they're gone!"

Ruth Rose looked toward the clubhouse. "Maybe Mr. Pocket moved them someplace else when the game started," she said.

Josh was shaking his head. "No! The glass case is smashed in a million pieces," he said. "Someone stole those balls!"

Dink and Ruth Rose stared at Josh openmouthed.

"Should we tell Mr. Pocket?" Ruth Rose asked after a few seconds.

"We have to," Dink said.

"He'll go bonkers!" Josh predicted.

The three kids walked over to Mr. Pocket.

Dink swallowed, then tugged on the man's arm.

"Hi there," Mr. Pocket said. "Where's that ump? These people want some baseball action!"

"Um, did you do anything with those six baseballs?" Dink asked.

"Why, of course," Mr. Pocket said. "You saw me lock them in the case."

"You didn't move them anywhere else?" Ruth Rose asked.

Mr. Pocket's smile vanished. "What's going on, kids? Has something happened to my baseballs?"

"They're gone!" Josh said. "The case is smashed. There's glass all over the floor!"

Mr. Pocket turned and marched toward the clubhouse.

The three kids watched him go.

"You didn't happen to see Pete when you went inside, did you?" Ruth Rose asked Josh.

"Nope. The first thing I saw when I got inside was all the glass," Josh said. "I was the only one in the place."

"Gosh," Dink said, "do you think Pete stole Mr. Pocket's baseballs?"

CHAPTER 3

Officer Fallon left his position on the field and walked over to the kids. "What's going on?" he said. "Where's our umpire?"

"We don't know," Josh said. "But Mr. Pocket's baseball collection is missing!"

Officer Fallon blinked. "What do you mean, 'missing'?" he asked.

Josh told Officer Fallon what he'd discovered.

"Did you see anyone else inside the clubhouse?" the police chief asked.

Josh shook his head. "I was the only one there," he said.

Officer Fallon looked toward the clubhouse. "Pete went inside just before you did, Josh," Officer Fallon said. "Are you telling me he wasn't in there?"

Josh shook his head. "I didn't see anyone. After I noticed the baseballs were gone, I got the heck out of there!" he said.

Mr. Pocket stormed up to them. His face was as white as his hair. "They *are* gone!" he said.

"Thaddeus, just how much are those balls worth?" Officer Fallon asked.

"A great deal," Mr. Pocket said. "But I don't care about the money. My father gave me those baseballs."

"I'll do my best to get them back for you," Officer Fallon said. He ran toward the parking lot, where he'd parked his cruiser.

Mr. Pocket sighed. "Well, I guess the game is over," he said. He walked away. A minute later, the kids heard his voice over the public-address system. "LADIES AND GENTS, I'M SORRY TO REPORT THAT THE GAME HAS BEEN CALLED OFF."

There was a pause. Then he continued: "WE HOPE THE GAME WILL BE CONTINUED IN A FEW DAYS. WE'LL LET YOU KNOW AS SOON AS WE KNOW MORE. THANK YOU."

The kids watched Mr. Pocket walk toward Main Street.

The people in the bleachers began leaving. Dink could hear their disappointed voices as they passed. The men straggled off the field, looking confused.

Ellie walked over to the kids. "What's that all about?" she asked. "And what's with Mr. Pocket? After he talked with you kids, he looked like he swallowed some nails!"

Josh explained.

"And Pete disappeared the same time the baseballs did!" Ruth Rose added.

"You're kidding, right?" Ellie said.

"Nope. Officer Fallon just took off," Josh said. "I think he's going to try to find Pete."

Ellie looked sad. "Gee, he seemed like such a nice guy," she said.

"I thought so, too," Dink said.

"Do you know where he came from?" Ruth Rose asked Ellie. "I mean, we don't really know anything about him."

"All I know is what he told me a couple days ago," said Ellie. "He came into the diner for a coffee and we chatted. He said he was heading down south, but he stopped to earn some more money. He's got a trailer parked at the river campground."

"But where did he come from?" asked Dink.

Ellie shrugged. "Didn't say. But I find it hard to believe that he's a thief."

"You know what's weird?" Josh said.

"If Pete planned to steal the balls, why'd he do it during the game?"

"Maybe he figured no one would be in the clubhouse," Ruth Rose said. "I guess he was right!"

"It seems awfully strange," Ellie said. "Well, if the game is off, I'd better get back to my diner."

Ellie hurried away, and the kids walked slowly toward Main Street. A lot of people stopped them to ask what was going on. The kids explained, and the people went away shaking their heads.

Just as the kids reached Main Street, Officer Fallon's cruiser appeared.

In the backseat, staring straight ahead, sat Pete Unkenholz.

GREEN LAWN POLICE

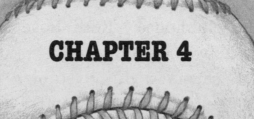

CHAPTER 4

"Did you see that?" Dink asked. "Officer Fallon arrested Pete!"

"Let's go see what's going on!" suggested Josh. "Do you think they'll put him in jail?"

The kids hurried up West Green Street. Just as they passed the elderly-housing apartments, they saw Officer Keene pulling up in a black truck. He parked it in front of the police station and stepped out.

"That's Pete's truck!" whispered Josh.

"Hello, Officer Keene," Dink said.

"What's going on? Is Pete under arrest?"

Officer Keene nodded. "We caught him in his truck. Pete admitted he took those baseballs," he said.

"Did you get them back, Officer Keene?" Ruth Rose asked.

"Nope. Pete told us he stole 'em but won't say what he did with 'em," Officer Keene said. He hurried into the police station.

The kids sat on the front steps.

"Gee, what a mess," Josh said. "Poor Mr. Pocket finds an umpire who ends up stealing his baseballs!"

"Guys, something's not right about this," Dink said. "Why would Pete confess to stealing the baseballs, then not tell what he did with them? I mean, why not just lie and say he didn't steal them?"

"Something else doesn't make sense," Ruth Rose added. "Why would Pete steal the balls when hundreds of people watched him go into the clubhouse for his allergy medicine? Everyone would *know* he was the thief!"

Dink shook his head. "I don't know. It's hard to believe a guy who helped us set up the bleachers would turn around and steal from us," he said.

"Then why did he say he stole the baseballs?" Josh asked.

Dink stood up. "I wish we could talk to Pete," he said. "Maybe he saw someone else in the clubhouse. Gosh, he might even have seen someone take the baseballs!"

"And maybe that's why he's not talking," Ruth Rose added. "The crook might be somebody he knows!"

"Pete Unkenholz just got to Green Lawn," Josh said. "He doesn't know anyone here."

After a minute, Ruth Rose said, "No one here knows him, either. Pete could be a bank robber for all we know!"

"I wish we knew more about him," Dink said.

"I just thought of something!" Ruth Rose cried. "If we do an Internet search, we might learn something about Pete."

"That's a good idea," Dink said. "Let's go talk to Mrs. Mackleroy!"

They crossed the street and walked into the library. The librarian, Mrs. Mackleroy, was sitting at her computer.

"Hi, kids," she said. "What a disappointment that the game was canceled!"

The kids told her about Pete's arrest.

"What?" she said. "He certainly doesn't seem the type to steal."

"Officer Keene said Pete confessed," Josh told her.

Mrs. Mackleroy shook her head. "My goodness," she said. "Well, how can I help you kids today?"

"We think there's something fishy

going on," Dink said. "It just doesn't make sense that Pete would steal those balls during the game."

"We want to search on the Internet to see if we can find out more about him," Ruth Rose said.

"I'm not sure what kind of information we'd get," Mrs. Mackleroy said. "But let's try a quick search. I was just on YuBuy. My husband's birthday is coming up, and I decided to shop online."

She closed out of YuBuy and opened up a search engine. "Do you know Pete's last name?" she asked.

"It's Unkenholz," Dink said, and spelled it for her as she typed.

A window opened on her monitor. "Hmph, they're telling me no Pete or Peter Unkenholz was found."

"Why don't you try just the last name?" Ruth Rose suggested.

"Good idea, hon," Mrs. Mackleroy said, typing in just *Unkenholz*. This time she got results. There was a link to the Web site for the *Coast Press* newspaper in Penobscot, Maine. The kids leaned closer to the monitor and read:

Penobscot, Maine, December 10
Reported by Susan Greene

BAKERY VAN STOLEN

Marion Unkenholz admitted taking a local baker's delivery van for a joyride. The van's owner, Arnold Sugar, decided not to press charges.

CHAPTER 5

"Who's Marion Unkenholz?" asked Josh.

"I wonder if she's related to Pete," Dink said.

"I think *Marion* is a man's name," Mrs. Mackleroy said. "The female *Marian* has an *a* instead of an *o*."

Ruth Rose glanced at the monitor again. "The reporter who wrote the story is Susan Greene. Maybe she knows this Marion Unkenholz. Could we call her?"

Mrs. Mackleroy picked up her phone and dialed information. She asked for the *Coast Press* in Penobscot, wrote down the number, and handed the phone to Ruth Rose.

Ruth Rose punched in the number, then listened. A second later, she asked to speak to Susan Greene.

After a pause, she said, "Well, is there anyone else who can tell me anything about Marion Unkenholz? Your paper reported that he stole a van."

Ruth Rose waited and then listened to someone else. "It is?" she said. "Oh. Well, thank you."

Ruth Rose handed the telephone back to Mrs. Mackleroy.

"Susan Greene moved to California," she said. "But I spoke with another reporter. He remembered the stolen van because his sister works in Sugar's Bakery."

"Did you find out if Pete is related to Marion?" Josh asked.

Ruth Rose nodded. "Pete *is* Marion," she said.

"Huh?" said Josh.

"The reporter said the thief's full name is Marion *Peter* Unkenholz," Ruth Rose said. "I guess he goes by Pete."

Dink just blinked at the news. He felt numb. "Could it be a different Pete Unkenholz?" he asked.

Josh grinned. "Yeah, like there are a bunch of Unkenholzes running around in Pen . . . that place in Maine."

"I'm sorry you had to get this bad news," Mrs. Mackleroy said. She took her purse from a drawer. "You're welcome to stay, but I have to get some lunch now."

"Us too," Josh said. He looked at Dink and Ruth Rose.

"Okay," Dink said. "I don't know what else we can do."

"Well, I have an idea," Ruth Rose said.

The kids thanked Mrs. Mackleroy and left the library.

"Does your idea have anything to do with lunch?" Josh asked Ruth Rose. "I'm so hungry I could eat a spider!"

Ruth Rose headed down West Green Street. Dink and Josh shrugged, then followed her across Main Street.

"Where are we going?" Dink asked.

"To the river," Ruth Rose said, heading past the empty baseball field. "I want to check out Pete's trailer."

"Why?" asked Josh.

"Because I don't believe Pete is the

kind of person who would take someone's van for a joyride," Ruth Rose said.

"But you just told us that reporter said Pete did it!" Josh said.

Ruth Rose shook her head. "I just have a feeling there has to be some other explanation," she said.

"I guess I agree," Dink said. "It almost seems like Pete is two different people."

The kids followed a sunny path toward the river. In a clearing they saw picnic tables and fireplaces. Only one campsite was occupied. Under a tree was a small white trailer, the kind you pull behind a car or truck. A few yards away the Indian River sparkled in the sunlight.

"Cool trailer," Josh whispered. "It would be fun to sleep here. You could fish from your bed!"

Three aluminum steps led up to a door. Under a window was a lawn chair.

A red-and-blue flannel shirt was draped over its back.

The spot was quiet except for bird-calls and squirrels scampering in the leaves.

Josh picked up the shirt, then put it back on the chair. "How do we know if this is Pete's trailer?" he asked.

Dink walked around the trailer. "I think it is," he said. "Look at this."

Josh and Ruth Rose followed him. Dink pointed to the license plate. It was from Maine.

Josh walked up the steps and rapped on the door. "Anybody home?" he called.

When no one answered, he tried the doorknob. "Locked," he said.

Dink stood on the lawn chair and tried to look through the window next to the door. "There's a curtain," he said.

Ruth Rose walked over to the picnic table. There was a trash barrel and a small stone fireplace with a grill for cooking. A long-handled fork was resting on the edge of the fireplace.

Ruth Rose picked up the fork and poked at the stuff in the trash barrel.

"Hungry?" Josh cracked, walking toward her with Dink.

Ruth Rose stuck the fork into a small box and pulled it out of the barrel. On the side of the box was a picture of a man sneezing.

Below the picture were the words ALLER-GREEN. FAST RELIEF FROM GRASS ALLERGIES.

MAXIMUM STRENGTH

KER-CHOO!

Aller-Green

FAST RELIEF FROM GRASS ALLERGIES

CHAPTER 6

"Pete wasn't faking his allergies!" Dink said.

"So he *was* going into the clubhouse for his medicine," Josh said.

"We have to show this to Officer Fallon!" Ruth Rose said, shoving the box into her pocket.

The kids ran almost all the way to the police station. They hurried up the front steps and down the cool hallway and knocked on Officer Fallon's door.

"Come in!" he said.

When the kids entered, Officer Fallon was just hanging up the phone.

"Hey, kids," the police chief said. "Looks like you've been running. Have a seat and catch your breath."

Ruth Rose put the Aller-Green box on his desk, and the kids sat down. "We found that at the campsite!" she said. "This proves Pete really *does* have allergies!"

Officer Fallon held up a large hand. "Whoa, slow down," he said, smiling at Ruth Rose. "What campsite?"

"We found out Pete is living in a trailer at the campground," Dink explained. "So we went there, and Ruth Rose found the box in the trash."

Officer Fallon picked up the box. As he read the print, the kids explained how they'd found the article about Pete on the Internet.

"We found out he . . ." Josh stopped and looked guilty.

"What, Josh?" Officer Fallon said. "What were you going to say?"

"Well, we found out that Pete stole a van," Josh said.

Officer Fallon set the medicine box on his desk. "Anything else?" he asked.

"His first name is really Marion," Ruth Rose went on. "He comes from Penobscot, Maine. I called the newspaper, and a reporter told me his middle name is Peter."

Officer Fallon rubbed his chin. "You've been busy," he said.

"We don't think Pete stole anything!" Ruth Rose said.

"We think he went inside to get his medicine, not to steal Mr. Pocket's baseballs," Dink added.

"Or maybe the medicine made a good excuse to go into the clubhouse," Officer Fallon said. "Remember, Pete confessed to taking the balls."

Officer Fallon stood up and walked over to his office window. "Why would he confess to something he didn't do?" he asked over his shoulder.

"He might have seen another person

in the clubhouse," Josh volunteered. "Maybe he's protecting someone."

"Maybe. All I know is, Pete is unwilling to talk to me," Officer Fallon said. "He shut up like a clam."

"How long will Pete have to stay in jail?" Ruth Rose asked.

The chief sighed and slumped into his chair. "I'm afraid Pete could go to prison for a very long time," he said.

No one said anything for a minute.

"What if we found the baseballs?" Dink asked. "If Mr. Pocket got them back, could Pete get out of jail?"

"A judge would have to decide that," Officer Fallon said. "There will be a trial. I've been trying to get a lawyer for Pete."

"Did you find one?" Dink asked.

"Yes," Officer Fallon said. He tapped a pencil against the Aller-Green box. "But when I asked Pete, he said he wouldn't speak to her."

CHAPTER 7

"But why not?" Josh asked.

Officer Fallon shook his head. "I wish I knew," he said. "If anyone ever needed a good lawyer, Pete does."

"Could we visit Pete?" Dink asked. "We could try to convince him to talk to the lawyer."

Officer Fallon gazed at Dink across his desk. "We have nothing to lose," he said finally. "I'll take you three to his cell for a few minutes. Explain to Pete that he needs a lawyer!"

The kids followed Officer Fallon out of his office, along a hallway, and down a set of stairs. At the bottom, Officer Fallon opened a steel door.

Behind the door was a large, windowless room. In one corner, iron bars formed a small cell. Inside the cell, Pete Unkenholz sat on a chair, staring at his feet.

"I brought you some company," Officer Fallon said. He nodded at the kids and left the room.

Pete looked up. He licked his lips but didn't say anything. His eyes looked scared.

"How are you?" Ruth Rose asked.

Pete shrugged. "Fine," he said in a soft voice.

"Do you have your allergy medication?" Dink asked.

Pete nodded his head toward a box of Aller-Green that stood on a small table.

"Officer Fallon really wants to help you," Josh said. "He found you a good lawyer. Will you talk to her?"

Pete licked his lips again. "Look, I appreciate your coming, but I already told them I took the balls," he said.

"But you need a lawyer!" Ruth Rose said. "And we don't think you took those baseballs, even if you said you did!"

Pete's eyes widened, but he didn't say anything.

"When you went to the clubhouse for your medicine, did you see anyone else there?" Josh asked.

Pete shook his head. "I stole the baseballs," he muttered.

"But why won't you tell Officer Fallon where they are?" Dink asked. "And why won't you talk to the lawyer?"

Pete twisted in his chair so his back was to the kids. "Please just go away," he said over his shoulder.

After a few seconds, the kids left. They walked back to Officer Fallon's office.

"Any luck?" the police chief asked.

"He told us to go away," said Josh.

"Thanks for trying," Officer Fallon said. "Maybe Pete just needs more time to think."

The kids left the police station and headed toward Main Street.

"Now I'm really confused," Ruth Rose said. "It's almost like Pete *wants* to stay in jail."

"Something else has been bugging me," Josh said. "If Pete did steal the balls, why didn't he just hide them, then come back to the game? By leaving the way he did, he practically pointed a finger at himself."

Ruth Rose rubbed her temples. "My brain is tired," she said.

"Your brain needs peanut butter," Josh said. "It's a scientific fact that when your brain is stuck, you need something even stickier to get it unstuck! Peanut butter!"

Dink and Ruth Rose both shoved

Josh. But they were hungry, so they followed him to his house on Farm Lane.

Josh's mother was in the kitchen, still dressed in shorts and sneakers. She was looking through the window at Josh's younger brothers in the backyard.

"You made a great catch today, Mrs. Pinto!" Ruth Rose said.

Josh's mother smiled at the kids. "It was just luck," she said. "The ball came right to me. Any news about Mr. Pocket's baseballs?"

The kids quickly told her what they'd learned about Pete.

"Goodness!" Josh's mother said. "Pete Unkenholz seems like the most honest person in the world!"

She headed out of the room. "Will you watch the boys while I shower?" she asked Josh.

"Sure, and we're gonna make sand-wiches, okay?" Josh asked.

"Okay, and send your brothers in for their lunch in a few minutes," his mother said as she climbed the stairs.

Josh made thick peanut butter sandwiches while Dink and Ruth Rose found the milk and three glasses.

They ate outside at the picnic table. Josh's twin brothers were playing with his dog, Pal, on the lawn.

The two four-year-olds were tugging on one end of an old T-shirt. The other end was in Pal's mouth.

The boys laughed and yelled. Pal growled and tossed his head back and forth. All three were covered with dirt.

"Mom's gonna flip out when she sees what you're doing to your shirt!" Josh yelled.

"It isn't our shirt!" Brian yelled back.

"It's yours!" Bradley chimed in.

Both boys burst into giggles and went running after Pal.

Dink and Ruth Rose laughed.

"Bye-bye, shirt," Dink said.

"Probably one of my favorites, too," Josh muttered.

Then he jumped up and nearly spilled his milk.

"Guys, there was a shirt at Pete's trailer," he said. "Outside on that chair."

"We saw the shirt," Ruth Rose said, licking peanut butter off her fingers. "So?"

"I picked it up," Josh went on. "At the time I didn't think anything about it. But now I realize that shirt is way too small to fit Pete. It must belong to someone else."

"Like who?" Dink asked.

"I don't know," Josh said. "But if Pete's not talking, maybe we can talk to whoever owns that shirt!"

"If we can find him," Dink said.

"Or her," Ruth Rose added.

"Pal might be able to help," Josh said. He whistled, and his dog came trotting from behind the barn, quickly followed by Brian and Bradley.

Pal flopped on the ground and plopped both front paws on top of the wet, filthy T-shirt.

"Mom wants you guys inside for lunch. And you'd better wash your hands," Josh told Brian and Bradley. "They're gross!"

"Uh-uh, they're clean!" Bradley said. He and his brother held up four dirty hands.

Josh leaned toward his little brothers. "Mom's making you a surprise for lunch!" he whispered.

"Yay!" screamed Brian, heading for the door.

"Wait up!" yelled Bradley as he raced after his brother.

"Come on," Josh said to Dink and Ruth Rose. He clipped Pal's leash to his collar and tossed the ruined T-shirt onto the picnic table. Then they all headed back to the campsite.

Five minutes later, they saw the trailer. Pal spotted a squirrel and began barking and tugging on the leash.

The squirrel dashed up a tree as the kids approached the trailer.

"Nobody's here," Ruth Rose said,

glancing around the clearing.

"Well, someone has been," Josh said,
pointing to the lawn chair. "The shirt is
gone!"

CHAPTER 8

"I wonder who took it," Dink said.

Ruth Rose climbed the steps and knocked on the door. "Anyone in there?" she called out.

The trailer remained silent. Pal sniffed the ground near the chair, then began whimpering. He sat facing the trailer and wagged his tail.

"Pal smells someone," Josh said.

"Should we wait around?" Dink asked.

"I can't think of anything else to do," Ruth Rose said, sitting on an aluminum step. "The game is canceled, Mr. Pocket's baseballs are missing, and Pete's in jail."

Suddenly the trailer door burst open. A boy appeared with a wild look in his eyes. He resembled Pete Unkenholz, only a lot younger. His blond hair was messed up and he was wearing the flannel shirt.

"What do you mean, 'Pete's in jail'?" the kid demanded.

Pal let out a low bark. "Hush, Pal," Josh said.

Ruth Rose was so startled she jumped off the steps. "Who . . . who are you?" she stammered.

The boy shook his head. "You first. Who are you guys?"

Dink took a step toward the boy. "I'm Dink and these are my friends Josh and Ruth Rose," he said.

The boy studied the group. "I saw you at the game," he said, raking a hand through his hair. "I'm Buddy, Pete's brother. Is he really in jail? Why?"

"He stole . . . I mean, the cops think he stole some valuable baseballs," Josh said.

Buddy just stared with his mouth open. "The baseballs in that glass case," he said. "Pete showed them to me before the game started. But he didn't take 'em. My brother wouldn't steal a penny."

"But he confessed," Dink said.

Buddy came through the door and flung himself down on the top step. "He must be lying for me so the cops won't think I stole the balls."

Dink stared at Buddy. He looked around fourteen years old. His eyes were red, as if he'd been crying. "Did you take them?" Dink asked.

Buddy shook his head. "Heck, no," he muttered. He swallowed and took a deep breath. "But Pete must think I did."

"Why would he think that?" Ruth Rose asked.

"Because I was teasing him before

the game," Buddy said. "We were both looking at the balls, and I said something stupid like 'I'll bet we could get a lot of money for these.'"

Buddy looked up. "It was just a joke. Pete's fun to tease," he said. "Anyway, I saw Pete leave the game to go after his medicine. When he didn't come back, I went inside to see if he was okay. But Pete wasn't there. The glass case was busted and the balls were missing. I figured Pete must have thought I stole 'em and came to the trailer looking for me. So I ran back, but Pete wasn't here."

"Officer Fallon picked up Pete in his truck," Dink said. "That's when your brother said he took the balls."

"Yeah, to keep me out of trouble," Buddy muttered. "Just like he did before we left Maine."

"What happened in Maine?" Ruth Rose asked Buddy.

"Something really dumb," Buddy

said. He stared into the trees that surrounded the clearing.

"Pete and I live together because our folks died in a car crash a few years ago," Buddy said. "Ever since then, I keep messing up and Pete keeps trying to get me out of trouble."

Buddy scooted down the steps and reached out to pet Pal. The dog licked Buddy's hand and rolled over on the ground.

"Last winter I was hanging out with my friend Fizzo," Buddy said. "Pete doesn't like Fizzo. Says he's a bad influence on me. Anyway, it was cold, and we saw this delivery van in the alley next to Sugar's Bakery. The engine was running, and Fizzo says, 'Let's sit in it to get out of the cold.' We sat there for a few minutes, smelling the warm bread. Next thing you know, Fizzo's driving the van."

Buddy looked up at Dink, Josh, and

Ruth Rose. "It was just supposed to be a joke on Mr. Sugar," he said. "Fizzo wanted to park the van around the corner, for laughs. Only the road was icy, and the van slid into a snowbank. Fizzo got out to try to shove us free. I slipped behind the wheel to put the van in reverse. That's when the police came, and we got busted."

"So . . . Pete didn't take the van?" asked Ruth Rose.

"No way!" Buddy shouted. "I told you, my big brother's the most honest guy in the world."

Buddy stroked Pal's silky ears. "Anyway, Fizzo and I are at the police station, scared to death," he continued. "I called Pete and told him what happened. Five minutes later, he came flying into the police station."

Buddy shook his head. "I still can't believe what happened next. Pete lied, probably for the first time in his life. He told the police officers he was the one who drove the van into the snowbank. Pete said, 'The whole thing was my idea. I took the van, not my little brother or Fizzo.'"

The three kids just stared at Buddy.

"When they asked Pete to explain why only Fizzo and I were in the van, Pete said he panicked and ran," Buddy went on. "They believed him. Then Fizzo's folks came to get us, and Pete sat in jail overnight."

Buddy scratched Pal's belly and the dog let out a big sigh. "Don't you see? Pete's lying for me again," Buddy said. "I don't know who took those baseballs. But it wasn't me, and it sure wasn't Pete!"

CHAPTER 9

"You have to tell Officer Fallon!" Ruth Rose said. "He has to let your brother out of jail now!"

"Okay. Let me lock up the trailer," Buddy said.

A few minutes later, the three kids headed over to the police station with Buddy. Pal led the way, snuffling his nose along the ground.

"Why did you and Pete leave Maine?" Josh asked Buddy.

The teenager shrugged. "After I got in trouble with Fizzo, Pete decided we should move to someplace new. We're headed south."

"What about school?" Dink asked.

"Pete's homeschooling me," Buddy said. "He's real smart."

"Why did you stop in Green Lawn?" asked Ruth Rose.

"We ran low on cash, so we stopped here for a while so Pete could earn more money," Buddy said as they walked. "He got a job painting a house about ten miles from here. Soon as he's done, we're supposed to head to Florida. Have you guys ever been there?"

"Yes, my grandmother lives in Florida," Ruth Rose said. She told Buddy about the gold mystery they solved the last time they visited her grandmother.

Soon they were standing in front of the police station. "Don't worry about Officer Fallon," Josh said. "He's a nice guy."

The kids climbed the steps. Josh tied Pal to a railing. "Stay and behave," Josh told his dog.

Pal woofed as the four kids walked into the building.

Ruth Rose knocked on Officer Fallon's door.

"Come in!" a voice said, and they trooped inside.

The police chief was sitting at his computer. He was staring at the screen and sipping from a mug of tea.

Officer Fallon glanced up. "Hello again. Who's this?" he asked, nodding at Buddy.

"This is Buddy Unkenholz," Dink said. "He's Pete's brother."

"Hello, young man," Officer Fallon said. He stood up and reached a long arm across his desk to shake hands.

"Is my brother okay?" Buddy asked.

"Yes, but he won't talk to me," Officer Fallon said. He pointed to the long sofa. "Have a seat, kids."

When they were lined up on his sofa, Officer Fallon smiled at Buddy. "You and your big brother look a lot alike," he said.

"Pete didn't take those baseballs," Buddy said.

"Oh? He insists he did," Officer Fallon said. "How do you know otherwise?"

"Pete must think I took those balls," Buddy said. "He's saying he did it so I won't get in trouble."

Officer Fallon tapped a pencil against his teeth and stared at Buddy. "Pete says he took the balls. You say he's lying to protect you. Who should I believe?" he asked.

"But my brother is honest!" Buddy blurted out. "He wouldn't steal anything. You can call anyone back home. They all call Pete 'Honest Abe'!"

Officer Fallon nodded. "I already made a phone call, to the police chief in

Penobscot, Maine," he said. "He told me about that van, and he said he's pretty sure your brother had nothing to do with it. Thing is, Pete insisted he was the one driving the van that night."

Buddy blushed. "That was me and Fizzo Martin," he said, looking at his feet. "Pete wasn't even there."

Officer Fallon stared at the unhappy boy. "So Pete lied to the Maine police about the van to protect you," he said. "And now you tell me he's lying again."

"Yes, sir," Buddy said. "But neither of us took those baseballs! Why can't you let him out of jail?"

Officer Fallon shook his head. "The baseballs are still missing. I'm sorry, son, but until they're returned and the thief is caught, Pete has to stay where he is."

CHAPTER 10

Buddy gasped. His eyes grew wide, and Dink thought he would start crying.

"Don't worry, Buddy. Pete will be fine till we get to the bottom of this," Officer Fallon said.

He looked at the troubled teenager. "But what are we going to do with *you*?"

"What do you mean?" Buddy asked.

"How old are you, son?" Officer Fallon asked.

"Fourteen," Buddy said. "But I'll be fifteen in three months!"

"Fourteen," Officer Fallon repeated.

"So I can't let you stay in that trailer alone."

Buddy glanced up with a sly look in his eyes. "So why don't you put me in jail with Pete?"

Officer Fallon laughed. "No, that won't do."

"He can stay with us," Dink said. "My folks won't mind. We've got a spare room."

Officer Fallon turned his gaze on Dink. "Are you sure?"

"I can call my mom and ask her," Dink said.

"Sound all right with you?" Officer Fallon asked Buddy.

"Sure, I guess," the boy said. He looked at Dink. "Thanks, man."

Officer Fallon handed his phone to Dink. Two minutes later, it was settled, and Dink hung up.

"Mom says Buddy can stay as long

as he needs to," he said. "She's getting two huge pizzas for tonight!"

"Cool!" cried Josh. Then he looked at Dink. "I'm invited, right?"

Dink nodded. "Ruth Rose, too. We'll have a party."

"Okay, why don't I drive you four to Dink's right now?" Officer Fallon asked.

"Can I go get my toothbrush and stuff?" Buddy asked.

Officer Fallon stood up. "Fine, we'll stop at the trailer first. Shall we go?"

Dink, Josh, Ruth Rose, Buddy, and Pal all climbed into Officer Fallon's cruiser. Buddy rode up front, and Pal lay sprawled across Josh's lap in the back.

It took only a minute to reach the quiet campsite. Officer Fallon parked near the picnic table.

"Buddy, I need to search the trailer before you go inside," Officer Fallon said.

"Search for what?" Buddy asked.

"As far as I can see, both you and
your brother had a chance to take the
baseballs," Officer Fallon said kindly. "I
want to believe you, but there are
too many unanswered questions about
those baseballs. If they're not in your
trailer, that's one question answered."

Buddy dug in his pocket, then
handed over the key to the trailer. "But
you won't find 'em," he muttered.

Officer Fallon climbed out of his cruiser. He strode to the trailer and used Buddy's key to let himself inside.

"He doesn't believe me," Buddy grumbled. He picked up a pinecone and tossed it at the trash barrel.

"Officer Fallon just wants to find Mr. Pocket's baseballs," Dink said. "They're really valuable."

"Well, he won't find them in our trailer," Buddy insisted.

"I believe you," Ruth Rose told Buddy. "If you and your brother didn't steal them, we have to find out who did!"

"Great, but how?" Buddy asked. "Anyone could have snuck into the club-house."

"But only people who came to the game knew the baseballs were in that glass case," Dink said.

"Oh my gosh!" Josh said. "The thief might live right here in Green Lawn!"

"Yeah," Dink grumbled. He was remembering the hundreds of people sitting in the bleachers. Was one of them the baseball thief?

"The first pitch was at eleven o'clock," Buddy said.

"What time did Pete go inside for his medicine?" Dink asked.

"It was around quarter past eleven," Buddy said. "Then I went looking for him a few minutes later. That's when I saw the smashed case and took off for the trailer."

"So that means someone stole the balls between eleven and eleven-fifteen," Ruth Rose said.

CHAPTER 11

Just then Officer Fallon walked out of the trailer.

"Thank you," he said, handing the key back to Buddy. "I'm happy to say that you were right and I was wrong."

"Can I get my stuff now?" Buddy asked.

"Sure, then I'll drop you all off at Dink's house."

Buddy climbed the aluminum steps and disappeared inside the trailer.

"Well, what do you think?" Officer Fallon asked the kids.

"I think he's telling the truth," Ruth Rose said.

"Me too," Dink and Josh said at the same time.

Officer Fallon raised his eyebrows. "Any particular reasons?"

"Well, if I were going to steal the baseballs, I wouldn't do it with all those people watching me walk into the clubhouse," Ruth Rose said. "And if I did take the balls, I'd hide them and return to the game so I didn't draw attention to myself."

"Could it have been Buddy?" Officer Fallon said, glancing at the trailer. "He could have stolen the balls and hid them till later."

"No," Dink said. "If Buddy were planning to take the balls, he wouldn't have teased his brother about stealing them. He'd want to keep his plan to himself."

"Besides," Josh said, "if Buddy did steal the baseballs, he wouldn't let his brother take the rap and sit in jail. Buddy really loves Pete."

"That's fine reasoning from all of you," Officer Fallon said. "And I'm inclined to agree with you. But then who *did* take the balls, and where are they now?"

"Could the thief sell the balls?" Dink asked.

"Oh, easily," Officer Fallon said. "There's a huge market for baseballs signed by famous players."

Just then Buddy opened the trailer door, locked it, and walked over to the picnic table. He was carrying a lumpy backpack.

"Get everything you need?" asked Officer Fallon.

Buddy nodded. "Will you tell Pete where I'll be staying?"

"I sure will, Buddy," Officer Fallon said.

They all climbed back into the cruiser. Five minutes later, Officer Fallon pulled up in front of Dink's house.

"Have a good pizza party," he said as the kids and Pal got out.

"Why don't you come, too?" Dink asked. "There will be plenty of food."

"Wish I could," Officer Fallon said. "But I need to begin talking to people who were at the game. Someone might have noticed whoever walked into the clubhouse just before Pete did."

"So you believe me?" Buddy asked.

Officer Fallon smiled. "I believe you," he said, then drove away.

"What time should we come over for pizza?" Josh asked Dink.

"How about five o'clock?" Dink said.

"Great! I have to muck out Polly's stall anyway," Josh said. "See you later!"

He and Pal headed up Woody Street toward Farm Lane.

"And I promised Nate I'd play with him, so I have to go, too," Ruth Rose said. "See you guys later."

Ruth Rose walked to her house next door.

"Your friends are nice," Buddy said as he followed Dink to his front steps.

Dink's mother opened the door. "Hello, Buddy," she said. "Come on in."

"Hello, Mrs. . . ." Buddy hesitated and looked at Dink. "I don't know your last name."

"I'm Mrs. Duncan," Dink's mom said. "And I've left a plate of cookies on the table."

Dink took Buddy upstairs and showed him the guest bedroom. "You can leave your pack here," Dink said.

Buddy knelt down and looked into Loretta's cage. The guinea pig squeaked and stood on her hind legs.

"I wish I could have a pet," Buddy said. "But Pete says we'll have to wait till we're not living in that tiny trailer."

"Are you guys really going to Florida?" Dink asked as they walked back downstairs and into the kitchen.

Buddy shrugged. "I don't know," he said. "I kind of like it here in Green Lawn."

Dink poured two glasses of milk and handed one to Buddy. "We've got a real good high school," he said, taking a cookie.

"Do they have a soccer team?" Buddy asked.

"Big-time!" Dink said.

Buddy smiled and helped himself to a cookie.

CHAPTER 12

Josh rubbed his stomach. "I think I'm going to explode," he said.

"Gee, why?" asked Ruth Rose, eyeing the two empty pizza boxes on Dink's picnic table. "You only ate ten pieces."

Josh fed his last crust to Pal under the table. "Nine pieces," Josh said, grinning at Dink. "I wanted to save room for dessert."

"There is no dessert," Dink said. "Not until we find out who took those baseballs."

"I wonder if Officer Fallon had any luck," Ruth Rose said.

"Maybe the crook already sold them," Josh said.

"Where would he sell them?" Dink asked.

"Well, if it were me, I'd use the Internet," Buddy said. "The crook would reach millions of people at the same time."

"A lot of people shop online with YuBuy," Ruth Rose said.

"Yeah, they sell all kinds of stuff," Dink said. "Do any of you guys know how to use YuBuy? I sure don't."

"Me neither," Josh said. "But Mrs. Mackleroy does."

"The library closes at six," Ruth Rose said. "Why don't we go see her?"

Dink checked his watch. "We've got ten minutes. Come on!"

The four kids and Pal trotted to Main Street, then down to West Green Street. It was one minute to six when they ran up the library steps.

Mrs. Mackleroy was still sitting at her desk when they hurried inside. "Hi there. I was just getting ready to close," she said. "Do you need something?"

The kids introduced Buddy, then quickly explained their idea.

"And you think the thief would try to sell the baseballs on YuBuy?" she asked.

"It would be the fastest way, wouldn't it?" Buddy asked.

"Well, online shopping *is* fast," Mrs. Mackleroy said.

"Could we try?" Dink asked.

"Sure, why not?" Mrs. Mackleroy said. She booted up her computer, clicked on *Internet,* and typed in *YuBuy.com.* A few seconds later, they were all looking at YuBuy's home page.

"Look, there's a place to type in what you want to buy!" Josh said. "Should we type in *baseballs?*"

"That would give us too many

choices," Mrs. Mackleroy said. "How about we try *autographed baseballs*."

She typed in the words. Seconds later a window popped up telling her that there were about fifty possibilities.

"How do we choose?" Dink asked.

"We need to be more specific," Mrs. Mackleroy said. "Do you know whose signatures Mr. Pocket had?"

"One ball was signed by Babe Ruth," Ruth Rose said.

"Okay," said Mrs. Mackleroy. She scrolled back up and typed in *baseballs signed by Babe Ruth*.

A new window popped up. It said there was one Babe Ruth ball for sale.

Mrs. Mackleroy clicked, and there was a picture of a baseball. Babe Ruth's signature was clearly visible.

Next to the picture were these words: BUY THIS BASEBALL SIGNED BY THE GREAT BABE RUTH! OTHER AUTOGRAPHED BASEBALLS AVAILABLE!

"Does that look like it could be Mr. Pocket's ball?" Mrs. Mackleroy asked.

The four kids leaned closer to her computer screen.

"I don't know," Dink said.

"Why don't we call Mr. Pocket?" Ruth Rose suggested.

"We should also call Officer Fallon," Dink said. He pointed to the screen. "If this is the thief, Officer Fallon should be the first to know!"

"This is exciting!" Mrs. Mackleroy said, reaching for the telephone.

A few minutes later, Officer Fallon and Mr. Pocket hurried into the library.

Mr. Pocket put on his glasses and leaned close to the monitor.

"That's my baseball!" he announced.

"How can you tell?" Officer Fallon said, also peering at the picture.

"Look closely," Mr. Pocket said. "Right above Babe's signature there's a dent in the ball. That's where his bat struck. Babe Ruth signed this ball for my father personally."

Everyone moved closer to the screen.

"I see it," Officer Fallon said. "But a lot of used baseballs would have bat dents, wouldn't they?"

"But not in the same place," Mr. Pocket insisted. "If I held the ball in my hands, I'd be sure."

"Why don't you buy the ball?" Dink suggested to Mr. Pocket. "Have the thief mail it to you. Then, once you have it, Officer Fallon can arrest the guy and get your money back!"

"It won't work," Buddy said. "The guy'll be suspicious if someone who lives in Green Lawn tries to buy the ball. This is where he stole it!"

"Buddy's right," Officer Fallon said. "And our thief may very well live in this town. So what do we do?"

"I have a suggestion," Ruth Rose

said. "E-mail the guy, saying you want to buy the baseball. Then ask him where you should send the check."

"And if he really does live around here, you can go arrest him right now!" Dink said.

"Yeah," Josh said with a grin. "The dude will probably still be sitting at his computer when you ring his doorbell!"

They all looked at each other.

Then Officer Fallon nodded at Mrs. Mackleroy.

She clicked on a small window that said BUY IT NOW FOR $1,000. Under the window was a space to type a reply.

"A thousand bucks!" Josh squeaked.

"Okay, Mrs. Mackleroy, let's reel this fish in," Officer Fallon said.

Mrs. Mackleroy typed a message that said: *I wish to buy the Babe Ruth baseball. Please e-mail me your address, and I'll send $1,000 immediately. I may want to buy other balls as well.*

"Good job," Officer Fallon said.

Seven sets of eyes stared at the computer screen.

"Come on, take the bait," muttered Mr. Pocket.

A few seconds later, Mrs. Mackleroy checked her mailbox, and there was a message: *Send your check to Ted Gundy, 13 Boxwood Lane, Green Lawn, CT 06040.*

"Gotcha!" said Officer Fallon as he headed for the door.

CHAPTER 13

The baseball game continued on the following Saturday. Now it was the bottom of the ninth inning. The score was MEN 6, WOMEN 3. The women were at bat.

"Guess you're gonna owe me an ice cream cone," Josh teased Ruth Rose. "I think I'll have ten scoops."

"Think again," Ruth Rose said. "The bases are loaded, and Livvy's up. She's their best hitter!"

"Yeah, but there are two outs," Josh said. "If Livvy gets an out, the game's over and I win!"

"*If* she gets an out," Ruth Rose said.

While Dink watched Livvy Nugent practicing her swings, he thought about the last several days.

It had been an exciting time in Green Lawn. Officer Fallon had arrested the thief, Ted Gundy. The six stolen baseballs were found in his closet, and he went to jail.

"It's neat that Pete and Buddy are staying in Green Lawn," Josh said.

"Yeah, and Buddy told me that Officer Fallon had a long talk with Pete," Dink said. "He told him lying is wrong, even if it's done to protect someone else. But Pete really learned his lesson. Now Officer Fallon is trying to talk Pete into becoming a policeman!"

"Hush, you guys," Ruth Rose said. "We don't want to distract Livvy!"

Pete was signaling Livvy to step up to the plate. She tapped dirt out of her cleats and yanked her cap tighter.

Buddy had joined the men's team, and he was pitching. His first pitch was low, but Livvy swung and missed.

"STRIKE ONE!" bellowed Pete.

Buddy's second pitch was high. Livvy tried but missed again.

"STRIKE TWO!" Pete yelled.

By now everyone in the bleachers was standing. Some were rooting for the men, but most were chanting, "HOME RUN, HOME RUN, HOME RUN!"

Buddy wound up for the pitch. Suddenly everyone was quiet. The ball came right over the plate, right at Livvy's knees.

CRACK! The hit was a line drive just inside the first-base line. Livvy took off for first. Mrs. Mackleroy left first for second. Josh's mom tore away from second toward third.

Ellie shot away from third base and ran for home, where she got a huge

cheer. Then Josh's mom came in, followed by Mrs. Mackleroy.

"Tie game!" Ruth Rose yelled. Dink could barcly hear her. The crowd was screaming as Livvy dashed for home.

It was a grand slam! The game was over. The final score was WOMEN 7, MEN 6.

Josh slumped in his seat while Ruth Rosc did a little dance next to him.

"Well, who's up for an ice cream cone?" Dink asked, grinning at Josh.

"I am!" Ruth Rose said.

Dear Readers,

I received so many great suggestions for the U book title, including UNICORN, UMBRELLA, and UNCLE. But I finally decided on a baseball story because Matthew Johnson wrote to me and suggested that I use UMPIRE as part of my title. Thank you, Matthew.

From my readers, I get hundreds of letters and e-mails each week. Two questions I receive often are the following:

1. Where did you get the idea for the A to Z Mysteries?

2. Are Dink, Josh, and Ruth Rose real kids?

My original idea for this mystery series came from my own reading. I love to read good mystery books, so I decided to write mysteries for kids. Each book in this series has started with one idea. From that idea, I develop a problem and a setting. Then I add in characters, clues, and, finally, a solution to the problem. For every book in the series, I try to find a situation that kids would enjoy reading about.

Matthew Johnson

For example, the N book shows Dink, Josh, and Ruth Rose riding horses and panning for gold. In the E book, they learn about rare stamps. In *The Unwilling Umpire*, autographed baseballs get stolen, and the kids use a computer to help them in their search.

Dink, Josh, and Ruth Rose are not real—they are fictional characters. But maybe you know kids who are like them. I think kids like these three would make great friends.

My story ideas come from many places, but especially from reading. I hope you will *always* be readers!

Happy reading!

Sincerely,

Ron Roy

P.S. Please visit my Web site at www.ronroy.com!

Collect clues with Dink, Josh, and Ruth Rose
in their next exciting adventure,

THE VAMPIRE'S VACATION

"Josh, why would a vampire pick Green
Lawn for his vacation?" Dink asked.

But Josh wasn't listening. He had his
nose against the window. "There he is
again!" he shrieked.

The man in black was crossing Main
Street near the swan pond.

"Doesn't he look like a vampire to
you?" Josh asked Ellie.

Ellie didn't answer. She just backed
away from the window.

Turn the page for a sneak preview of

Who Cloned the President?

The first book in Ron Roy's exciting
new series, the Capital Mysteries!

Who Cloned the President?

the President?

by Ron Roy

1
KC's Discovery

KC Corcoran pulled a slip of paper out of her teacher's baseball cap. She read the words on the paper and grinned.

"Who did you get, KC?" Mr. Alubicki asked.

"President Thornton," KC said.

"No fair!" Marshall Li protested. "You already know everything about him."

Mr. Alubicki smiled and passed the hat to Marshall, KC's best friend. Marshall picked a slip. "Herbert Hoover?" he said. "I don't even know who he is!"

"But you'll know all about him after you write your report," his teacher said.

Mr. Alubicki finished passing the hat around the room. "Okay, everyone, have a great weekend. Get started on your president reports. We'll discuss them Monday."

KC grabbed her backpack and followed Marshall out the door. They walked home together every day.

KC and Marshall lived in the same ten-story building in Washington, D.C. It stood between a pet shop and a Chinese restaurant.

They stopped on the way home to watch puppies and kittens through the pet-shop window.

"Why is everyone so crazy about furry animals?" Marshall asked. "Spiders make great pets, too!"

KC laughed. "Marsh, you can't cuddle up with a spider."

"Who says you can't?" Marshall asked. "I wish Mr. A. would let us write about insects instead of presidents."

Marshall loved anything with more than four legs. He kept jars of crawly things in his bedroom. Spike, his pet tarantula, slept in one of Marsh's old baseball caps.

"Presidents' Day is in February," KC reminded her friend. "If we had an insects' day, Mr. A. would let you write about Spike."

"Spike's not an insect," Marshall said. "Tarantulas are spiders, and spiders are arachnids."

"I know, I know," KC said as she pushed open the glass door of their building. "You've told me a hundred times!"

"And you still don't remember,"

grumbled Marshall. He pushed the elevator button.

Donald, the building manager, opened the elevator door. Donald ran the elevator and helped people get taxis out front.

"Hi, kids," Donald said. "Got plans for the weekend?"

"We have to write reports," Marshall told him. "About dead presidents."

"Mine's not dead," KC told Donald. "I picked President Thornton!"

Donald smiled as he pressed the button for Marshall's floor. "Lucky you! Maybe you'll see him around town."

Marshall got off on the third floor, and Donald took KC to the fifth. She let herself into the apartment with her key.

Lost and Found, her two kittens, came skidding across the wood floor when the door opened. KC rubbed their bellies, then headed for the kitchen.

A note was taped to the fridge.

KC—I'll be home around six. Have a snack. Love, Mom.

KC grabbed a banana and walked into the living room. Lost and Found scurried after her. She pulled *Your Presidents* from a bookshelf and looked up President Thornton.

"Listen," she said to the kittens. "Zachary Thornton had five brothers and sisters. He raised chickens and sold eggs to help his family." Then the caption of a picture caught her eye. "As a Boy Scout, Zachary Thornton earned twelve merit badges," she read.

"See, Marshall was wrong," KC mumbled. "I don't know everything about

President Thornton. I had no idea he got twelve badges in Scouts."

KC marked the page, then switched on her mom's computer. She logged on to the Internet and found more about President Thornton. "Zachary Thornton is our fourth left-handed president," KC read.

"Cool. We're both left-handed!" KC said. She kept reading and noticed a headline from the *Washington Post* newspaper. "President Thornton Says No to Human Cloning."

KC read the rest of the paragraph about scientists cloning animals. Marshall had told her that some scientists wanted to clone humans.

"I'm glad the president said no," she said. "I only want one of me!"

KC shut off the computer and turned

on the TV. She flopped on the sofa and pulled the kittens onto her lap.

Cindy Sparks, the White House reporter, was just signing off.

"Someday that'll be me," KC told her kittens. She planned to become a TV anchorwoman after college.

KC peeled the banana and channel surfed. She found a live special on President Thornton at a press conference in the White House.

"Tomorrow morning," said President Thornton, "I will make an announcement that will change human life forever."

Then someone handed the president a stack of papers. He signed them slowly, as if he were tired. He didn't smile or talk to anyone around him. He just took a paper, signed it, and reached for another.

Hmmm, thought KC. *It's not like him to be so quiet and serious. He looks sick.*

KC noticed something else. "That's weird," she said. She called Marshall and told him to turn on channel 3.

"It's the president," Marshall said a few seconds later. "So?"

"Do you see anything weird?"

"Like what?"

"Marsh, he's signing those papers with his right hand!"

Marshall laughed. "You called to tell me the president is right-handed?"

"No, he's *left*-handed!"

"Oooh, let's call 911," Marshall said.

KC kept staring at the president on TV. Signing with the wrong hand. Looking tired and way too serious. Almost like a different person. . . .

Her imagination kicked in. What if this guy was a fake? What if the real president had been kidnapped? What if he'd been drugged or . . . KC shook her head.

She could almost hear her mom warning her—for the millionth time—not to jump to conclusions.

Then she remembered that headline: "President Thornton Says No to Human Cloning."

"That's it!" KC cried.

"Marshall, get up here right now!" she yelled into the phone. "Someone cloned the president!"

**Do you love the A to Z Mysteries?
Then check out Ron Roy's brand-new series
about KC and Marshall in Washington, D.C.!**

Capital Mysteries

When the President of the United States starts acting funny on TV, KC decides he's not the *real* President Thornton. She's sure he's a clone!

KC's mom and President Thornton have disappeared during the Cherry Blossom Festival. They were kidnapped—right under the bodyguards' noses!

Leonard Fisher claims he's the heir to the Smithsonian fortune. If KC and Marshall can't prove he's a liar, Washington will lose its world-famous museums!

A STEPPING STONE BOOK™

Great authors write great books . . .
for fantastic first reading experiences!

Grades 1–3

Adam Sharp series
  by George Edward Stanley
#1 The Spy Who Barked
#2 London Calling
#3 Swimming with Sharks
#4 Operation Spy School

Duz Shedd series
  by Marjorie Weinman Sharmat

Junie B. Jones series by Barbara Park

Magic Tree House® series
  by Mary Pope Osborne

Marvin Redpost series by Louis Sachar

Clyde Robert Bulla
The Chalk Box Kid
The Paint Brush Kid
White Bird

Jackie French Koller
Mole and Shrew Are Two
Mole and Shrew All Year Through
Mole and Shrew Have Jobs to Do
Mole and Shrew Find a Clue

Jerry Spinelli
Tooter Pepperday
Blue Ribbon Blues: A Tooter Tale

Grades 2–4

A to Z Mysteries® series by Ron Roy

Andrew Lost series by J. C. Greenburg

Capital Mysteries series by Ron Roy
#1 Who Cloned the President?
#2 Kidnapped at the Capital
#3 The Skeleton in the Smithsonian

Starvation Lake series by Gloria Whelan
#1 Welcome to Starvation Lake
#2 Rich and Famous in Starvation Lake
#3 Are There Bears in Starvation Lake?
#4 A Haunted House in Starvation Lake

Stephanie Spinner & Jonathan Etra
Aliens for Breakfast
Aliens for Lunch
Aliens for Dinner

Gloria Whelan
Hannah
Next Spring an Oriole
Night of the Full Moon
Shadow of the Wolf
Silver

NONFICTION
Magic Tree House® Research Guide
  by Mary Pope Osborne and others

Grades 3–5

The Magic Elements Quartet
  by Mallory Loehr
#1 Water Wishes
#2 Earth Magic
#3 Wind Spell
#4 Fire Dreams

NONFICTION
Thomas Conklin
The *Titanic* Sinks!

Elizabeth Cody Kimmel
Balto and the Great Race